BY THOMAS S. OWENS

Perfection Learning®

Cover and Inside Illustration: Holly Pendergast

Dedication

To "Uncle" John Crawford

About the Author

Thomas S. Owens is married to Diana Star Helmer, another author of children's books. Thomas is the author of more than 40 books, including *Collecting Basketball Cards* (Millbrook Press). He likes walking with Diana, cooking soups, gardening, watching cartoons, surfing the Internet, playing with Angel the cat, and living in Iowa.

Images used in this book come from Art Today.

Printed in the United States of America.
For information, contact
Perfection Learning® Corporation,
1000 North Second Avenue, P.O. Box 500,
Logan, Iowa 51546-0500.
Phone: 1-800-831-4190 • Fax: 1-712-644-2392
PB ISBN-10: 0-7891-5186-3 ISBN-13: 978-0-7891-5186-5
RLB ISBN-10: 0-7807-9440-0 ISBN-13: 978-0-7807-9440-5

8 9 10 11 12 13 PP 13 12 11 10 09 08

Table of Contents

CHAPTER

A Boy's Wish

JOHN ALEXANDER dropped a dead fish in every hole. The dirt he put back reshaped each mound.

John's father said rotting fish made the seeds grow. John thought only the smell grew.

"Father, when may I have a dog?" he begged.

John's father sighed. "Son, you know our village law. A poor man who cannot feed himself cannot feed a dog."

John started to kick one mound of dirt. He stopped. He knew that each mound had seeds for corn, beans, or squash. He kicked a nearby weed instead.

John watched his father's eyebrows rise. John suddenly wished he hadn't shown his anger.

"Young man, do not test my good spirits!" his father stated.

John stared at his father's dusty boots. That was better than looking at his stern frown or his wagging finger.

"John," his father began, "your life is just beginning. Farming is your future. This dog is all you think about. This could be your downfall."

John's father turned. There would be no more talk of a dog.

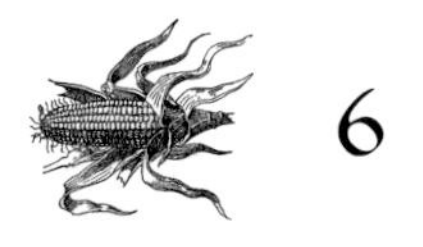

John headed for the stone fence. He hoped there might be a loose stone or two to throw.

The boy didn't watch his father head back to the house. But he heard the stomps. And he felt them.

"Doesn't he care about me?" John grumbled. "I work hard too! Why should I be alone? He can always be with Mother!"

John thought about the arguments with his father. There had been many.

Once John had watched a hungry black dog. It was wandering the countryside.

His father had insisted that if the dog were fed, it would never leave. "Food is too important to waste on strays!" he had warned John.

John had told his father that he'd eat less. Then the dog could have more.

John's father had screamed. "Don't be ungrateful, boy! Why must I have a sickly, starving son? One who wastes time on a worthless dog?"

John was sure his father had never known the joy of having a dog. Why did he have to grow up like his father had?

John put a pebble back on the stone fence. He could throw rocks later.

He was ready to talk about having a dog again. He would promise to train the dog. The dog could become a watchdog. It would guard the farm!

John ran to the cabin door. Before he could open it, he heard his mother crying. Had she argued with his father too?

The room seemed empty at first. Then John saw his mother. She was kneeling next to something covered with a sheet.

"Speak no more tonight," she warned. "Your father is dead."

CHAPTER 2

Two Alone

JOHN RAN outside. He looked to the sky. He wanted someone to listen. He wanted someone to believe he was sorry.

"Come back, John!" called his mother. "You don't understand."

But John understood. His mother had just told him. She said his father had come inside muttering, "Silly dog. Silly boy!" Then John's father had grabbed his chest and fallen to the floor.

Now John ran to an oak tree. He hugged the trunk and cried until he shook.

John wished he were hugging his father. He knew it was his fault. He had killed his father.

Mrs. Alexander caught up with her son. "He could have died at anytime, son," she said. "He had been working too hard."

John sobbed. "It's because I wasn't working hard enough!"

John's mother sighed. "No. Your father was old. He was past 40."

"What will we do now, Mother?" asked John.

She sniffed back tears. "Nothing until we bury your father."

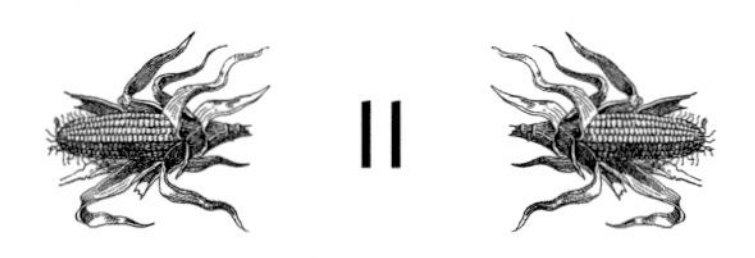

That night, Mrs. Alexander slept on a bit of hay next to the white sheet. She had left the body of John's father on the floor where it had fallen.

The next morning, neighbors took the body. A hole was dug. They buried Mr. Alexander. He was still wrapped in the white sheet.

Mrs. Alexander tied two sticks together for a cross. It marked the grave.

One by one, the neighbors filed by. The last one was a stranger. He was dressed better than any of the others. He also had a strong, sleek horse.

"Ma'am, I am Byron Bidwell," he boomed. "I am sorry about your husband's passing."

Mrs. Alexander whispered her thanks.

"However, I have something to tell you," the man continued. "Your husband died without repaying his debt. A year ago, he borrowed money from me. It is still owed."

John glared at the man. "What can we do, sir? My father is dead!"

Byron Bidwell sneered. "You can honor his word. Our contract says that the debt was to be repaid in one year. He signed the agreement."

Mrs. Alexander gritted her teeth. "That means we must repay the money. We don't have it. So the farm is yours."

Byron Bidwell inhaled. "There is a simple way to repay the money. You and your boy can work it out. In . . . say . . . three years. Then we would be even."

Mrs. Alexander wiped her eyes. "Do you mean we can send you money for three years?"

During colonial times, an **indentured servant** promised to work a certain amount of time for someone to repay a debt.

Byron Bidwell shook his head fast. His fat cheeks made a flapping sound. "No need to send me money, Mrs. Alexander. We'll see each other daily. You two will be **indentured servants**. MY servants!"

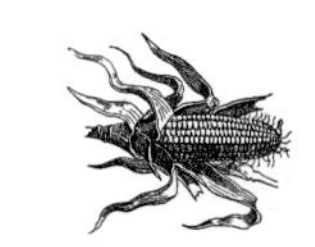

CHAPTER 3

A Life of Service

THE NEXT morning, Mr. Bidwell returned with a wagon.

"Don't worry. I'll sell the farm and what you leave behind," he stated. "The sale will lessen what you owe me."

John helped his mother onto the seat. He climbed into the back of the wagon. He found a place to sit among some flour sacks.

John turned his back on the only place he had ever lived. He couldn't look at his house one last time.

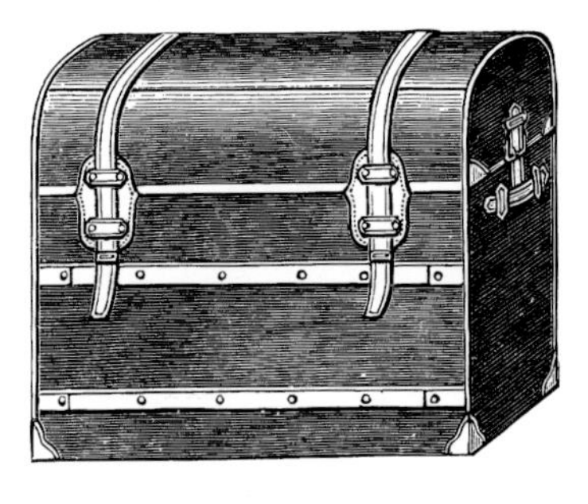

John faced the trunk. His mother had begged Bidwell to take the trunk along. She promised they would pack only clothing and a Bible.

Our whole life fits inside one small trunk, John thought. What room would a dog have in such a world?

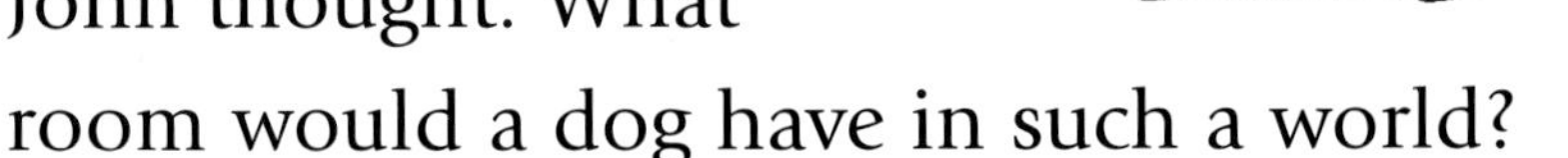

John knew they had only traveled a few miles. However, it seemed like entering another world. Before this, the longest trip he'd ever taken was to the village church.

The wagon topped a hill. John stared at the sight.

This was no small forest. This was a plantation. Tall trees hid the farm like a secret fence.

John smiled at the waiting house. His old house would disappear inside those walls.

Bidwell stopped the wagon.

He jumped down. "Let's be friends," Bidwell said as he helped John and his mother down. "What's your first name, Mrs. Alexander?"

John's mother paused. "Abigail. Why?"

"I will call you Abby!" he boomed. He turned to John. "You can call me Master Bidwell."

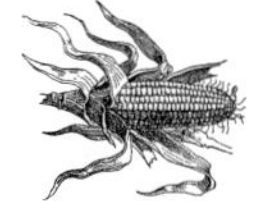

"Please, may we learn our jobs now?" John's mother asked.

Bidwell frowned. "Fine. You will cook and clean for me!" he grunted. "Young John will farm with me and care for my horses. Don't worry. I will correct your failings."

John's mother neared her master. John saw his mother squeeze both fists tight. "Sir, I signed a promise to work for you," she said. "I will do these jobs. But I will not serve as your wife. We are not married!"

Bidwell laughed. Then he wiped his large, sweaty face with a yellowed handkerchief. "You think too well of yourself, Abby," he said, still chuckling.

"I do want a wife. But not you! I want a young wife!"

"You keep an ordered house for me," he continued. "Then women will want to be part of my fine life."

John yanked on his mother's sleeve. She hushed him. But John spoke anyway. "Master Bidwell, which rooms will we live in?"

Bidwell's stomach shook hard from laughing. Tears rolled down his face. "I have a special place for you."

They walked to a small stable. John wondered how many horses were inside.

"This is where you will live, Lord Alexander!" Bidwell hissed. "My horses have a new home."

The stable door slammed. Mrs. Alexander leaned against a wall. She shook her head at their dark, dirty world.

"He treats us worse than two horses," John said.

"John, don't complain," his mother warned. "Your father survived this life. So can we!"

CHAPTER 4

The Working World

"WHAT DO you mean?" John asked. "What life did father live?"

Mrs. Alexander hid her face in her hands. "Your father begged me never to tell you," she whispered. "He had to pay his way from England. So he worked as an indentured servant on a Virginia farm for seven years. I didn't meet him until his service was done."

John put up both hands. He hoped to hold back the truth. "Noooo!" he blurted. "Father talked about his family. He talked about their hard lives."

John's mother showed a tiny, sad smile.

She reached for John's hand. "Son, those were the servants he lived with. He told me that he had to make his own family."

"His only real relative lived in England," John's mother continued. "It was his father. And he was very mean to him. Your father ran away from home when he was 12."

John flashed ten fingers. Then two more. "I am 12. He was just my age?"

John's mother nodded.

"Mother, does this mean that you too . . ."

She stopped him. "No, John," she began. "I wasn't a servant. My parents were traveling ministers."

"My mother would sing, and my father would preach," John's mother continued. "I was 14 when I met your father. My family never spoke to me again after our marriage."

John was quiet. "Because you loved a servant."

One tear trickled down his mother's cheek.

"I will not let us live like this, Mother!" John yelled.

John's mother choked back tears. "We have no choice, son," she sniffed. "I signed the contract. I signed for both of us. We have promised to work three years. In exchange, we have food, shelter, and clothing. And we will repay your father's debt."

John bent closer to his mother's lap. His knee banged against the dirt floor. "We can run away!"

His mother bit her lip. "We are good, Christian people," she said. "We have promised. Fear not, dear. We have only three years. Your father served seven."

John counted in his mind. He would be 15 years old when his service to Master Bidwell ended. He knew boys who never lived past 15. They died in farm accidents or from disease. So many fears awaited.

John stared at the ears of corn his mother was cleaning. She had been told to strip the kernels off the cobs. It had to be done by sunrise.

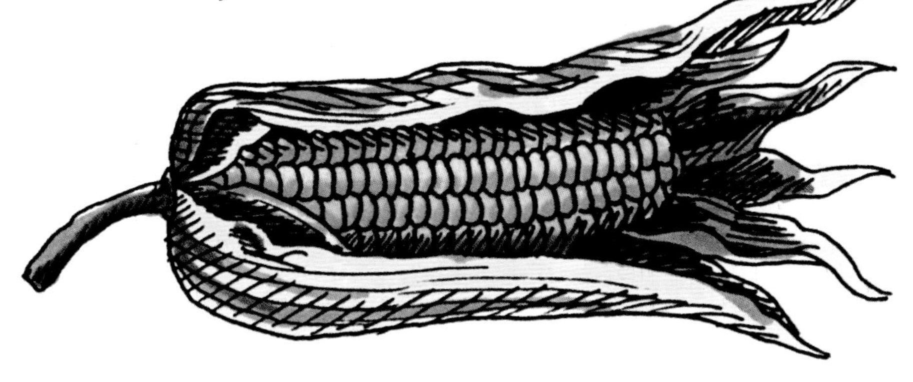

Mrs. Alexander told John to sleep while she finished.

But John grabbed an ear of corn. He yanked only two kernels off. He held them up.

"Master Bidwell thinks he owns us. But he doesn't!" John said. "We'll never be his belongings. We'll always be two seeds of hope."

CHAPTER 5

The Master Speaks

"GET UP, boy!" Bidwell shouted.

John leaped from his hay mattress. "What's wrong?"

"You are not working!" Bidwell said.

John pulled on his boots and hat. "Where is my mother?" he asked.

Bidwell growled. "She is working. I want corn bread for my night's meal. I sent her to the mill to have some cornmeal ground."

John nodded. Then he asked, "Did she take the wagon?"

"Not my wagon!" Bidwell chuckled.

"She walked?" John asked.

Bidwell placed his hand on John's shoulder. "If the lazy boy slept less, he could have done his mother's work. Besides, the mill is only a mile down the hill."

John blinked back tears. He staggered outside. There he saw a hoe and bucket waiting.

He worked beside Master Bidwell. John chopped tall weeds in the field. His father never let weeds get so large.

John didn't hear the bell ring. But he heard his mother.

"Lunch!" she called.

Bidwell dropped his hoe and headed for the house. John followed at a safe distance.

Mrs. Alexander held up a hand. John stopped before entering the master's kitchen. The boy watched from the doorway. His mother piled plates of food in front of the man he hated.

"Master, I brought the cornmeal from the mill," she reported. "You will have your corn bread tonight."

Like a greedy dog, Bidwell sniffed. "Hmmm!" he said. "I just hope it tastes as good as it smells. You may go."

John's mother curtsied and scrambled from the house. "We must eat quickly," she said to John.

There was no time to build a second fire for cooking. So the two ate carrots and apples. Hidden in Mrs. Alexander's apron pocket was dry bread. She had found it in Bidwell's pantry.

"Tell me about the mill," John said. He hoped his mother would think about something happier.

"The water from the stream pushes big wheels with great power," his mother said. "The wheels turn huge, flat stones. The stones crush the dried corn into cornmeal."

John patted his mother's hand. "I am sorry you had to carry the bags of corn yourself. I will try harder to help."

His mother laughed. "Well, I didn't have as much to carry home. Jameson Fox runs the mill. He usually keeps one pound of cornmeal that he grinds. It's his payment."

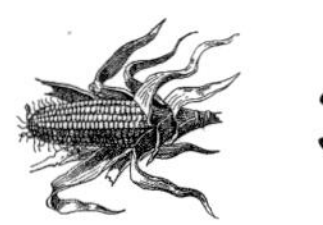

"But Mr. Fox was kind to me," she continued. "He said he takes two pounds if it's for Master Bidwell. That made two pounds less for me to carry."

John grunted. "It would teach Master Bidwell if the mill kept all the cornmeal! He makes me so angry that I could smash all the corn with my fists."

His mother smiled. But she didn't speak. She was too busy thinking. Would it work? she wondered.

CHAPTER 6

New Hope

MRS. ALEXANDER stopped drawing in the dirt. Her stick waved in the air as she talked.

"You did it, John!" she said. "When you talked of crushing corn with your fists, I saw the future."

John looked at the dirt. "I don't understand," he said.

"Fists are like hammers," his mother said. She pointed to her drawing.

"We need two wheels," she continued. "I could pump a foot pedal up and down. The force would turn one wheel."

Now John understood. He smiled. "And my fists would hit the spokes of the other wheel where the corn falls."

John's mother nodded. "Yes, just like making a **whetstone** turn with my feet."

John smiled. "No water power needed. Just foot power!"

John's mother yawned. "Enough of such dreams. It is time to sleep."

A **whetstone** is a wheel-shaped stone used to sharpen tools and knives.

John was tired too. He had spent all day in the field with Master Bidwell. But John had something to do before he could sleep. Only hope moved his feet as he ran to the mill.

John banged on the door of the mill.

"I am closed," came an answer.

"Sir. Please come with me at once. Your future is at stake!" John shouted.

A man opened the door. A white cloud of flour drifted around the mill owner. "I am Jameson Fox," he said. "Shall I call you Future Boy?"

John laughed. "You can call me anything. Just trust me, sir. Please come meet a great inventor. This person waits at the hilltop."

"We can meet next week," Fox said. "Most people sleep at night."

John placed one foot in the door opening. If the door closed, so did his

hope. “This new machine could replace your mill!” he bragged.

Fox frowned. He thought for a moment. “Very well. Show me my future.”

Soon, John and Mr. Fox reached Bidwell’s place. They went straight to the servants’ quarters.

Mrs. Alexander was sleepy and angry. “Son, I feared that you ran away,” she said. “What have you done? Has my boy wronged you, Mr. Fox?”

Fox laughed. "Your boy talked me into a visit. Future Boy's mother is the great inventor?"

John sighed. "Forgive me, Mother," he began. "Mr. Fox has to see your idea."

They explained the workings of a new corn grinder. Fox wrote more numbers in the dirt. He looked to the ceiling.

Finally, he smiled. "This can be a great machine," he said. "Every farm would buy one. You could be rich. And I can help."

"This dreaming should end now!" Mrs. Alexander cried. "My work belongs to Master Bidwell. My time does too. Why should I make him rich?"

John's eyes danced. "We sold our service once. Let us buy our service now."

Mrs. Alexander snorted. "Can you pull money from the air, young man?"

John shook his head. "The money we need comes from your mind. Here is my plan."

CHAPTER 7

Making It Work

THE NEXT morning, John knocked on Master Bidwell's office door.

"Come!"

John made sure not to smile. "Sir, may I please speak with you?"

Bidwell growled. "You? What have you done, boy? Tell the truth."

John bowed his head. "I want to make a deal with you, sir."

Bidwell flashed yellowing teeth. "A deal? I told your ma I won't marry her."

John glared. He swallowed his anger. "Forgive me, Master. I come to bring you good fortune."

Bidwell tipped his chair onto its back legs. He flopped his boots atop the desk.

John smelled a stink. The smell stuck to the bottom of his master's boots.

"Go on, boy!" Bidwell roared.

John nodded. "Sir, Mother and I cannot serve you well enough. You should sell our services."

Bidwell sucked his teeth. He rubbed his dirty beard. "Who would buy the two of you? A skinny boy and his homely mother."

Suddenly Bidwell slammed a fist on his desk. "Wait!" he barked. "Do you want to buy your own freedom? Never!"

John gulped. "Sir, it's not us. Jameson Fox from the mill could buy two servants. What if he asked?"

Bidwell sat up straight. He had a greedy look in his eyes. "Gaining Fox's favor could help business," he mumbled. "We could be partners in that mill."

"Sir?" John asked. "What did you say?"

"Um . . . nothing to you, boy!" Bidwell said. "I will visit Fox tomorrow. For 20 pounds of flour, I'd be delighted to be rid of you. All the money I want will come from the sale of your farm."

John's eyes grew wide. "You would trade us for nothing but flour? No money?"

Bidwell licked the last drops of wine from a bottle. "Foolish boy. Leave before I whip some respect into you."

John bowed. "Thank you so much."

John opened the door. Mrs. Alexander stepped in.

"What is this?" Bidwell sputtered. "You be gone too."

She curtsied. "I will, sir. With my boy. I heard we cost only 20 pounds of flour."

The wine bottle bounced on the floor. "You have tricked me. You will pay!" Bidwell screamed.

Jameson Fox stepped into the room. "I heard your offer too, Bidwell," he said. "I will come in the morning with the flour. And I will have a contract for you to sign. Then I'll remove these servants from your sight."

Bidwell clenched his fists.

Fox grabbed the fallen bottle. He lifted it into the air.

"But I'll let the judge take care of you," Fox continued. "We can prove how a selfish drunkard tried to cheat a mother and child."

Then he lowered the bottle.

Bidwell sat without moving. "The farm is still mine," he sneered.

John spoke up. "Farms or masters aren't in our future!"

CHAPTER 8

The New Day

JOHN RAN to the law office. His mother was signing a contract for her corn grinder. Mr. Fox was ready to start building and selling them.

Mr. Fox had paid Mrs. Alexander 10 **pounds** so far. That was enough money to rent rooms in the town inn. They could stay as long as they needed to.

A **pound** is a form of money. It was used in the early colonies. It is still used in England today.

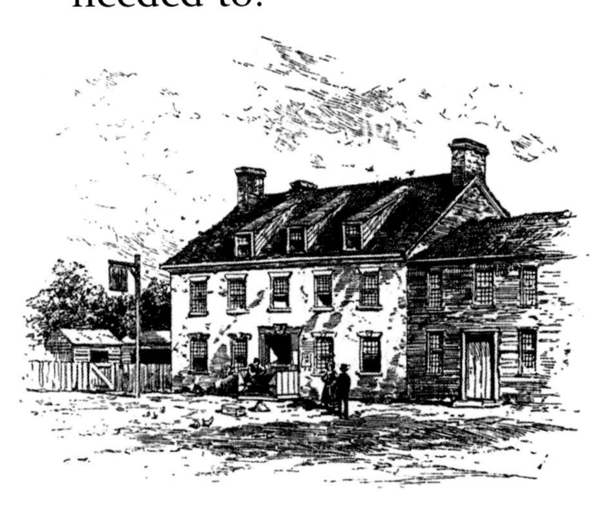

John's mother had made her son a promise. Soon they would make plans for a better future.

But John thought their future was now. "Mother, Mother!" he panted. "Have you heard about the Headright System? I ran all the way from the town square when I learned."

"Slow down! Breathe!" she ordered. "Let's sit down."

John's mother closed the lawyer's door. She and John sat on the steps to the office.

"Virginia offers 50 acres of land to anyone paying the passage from England for a servant!" John said. "We could spend our money for a farmworker. Then we would get free land to build a farm. And to build a home."

His mother scowled. "How did you feel when someone forced you to be a servant?" she asked. "Have you forgotten your blessings?"

John frowned. "Pardon me, Mother," he said. "Please don't accuse me of selfishness. Hear me out!"

NOVA BRITANNIA.
OFFERING MOST
Excellent fruites by Planting in
VIRGINIA.
Exciting all such as be well affected
to further the same.

LONDON
Printed for SAMVEL MACHAM, and are to be sold at
his Shop in Pauls Church-yard, at the
Signe of the Bul-head.
1609.

John's mother was silent. But she raised her eyebrows.

"We could have a rich life with only half that much land," he began. "Let's find a young man or young family. If they will farm our half of the land, we can give them the other half."

John continued, "We would be buying a partner. Not a servant."

John watched his mother's trembling lips. He added, "We've been given the gift of freedom. We have received. Now we can give. Isn't that what Father said?"

John's mother broke into a smile brighter than the sunrise. "Your father would be so proud," she said. "So am I. So proud I want to buy you a dog. Then we can have a simple life."

John threw back his head and laughed. "We have work to do."

John's mother scratched her head. "What work?"

John's smile was as big as his mother's. "We must open Alexander and Alexander. You are sure to invent many more machines besides a corn grinder."

John offered his mother his arm. She accepted. Tomorrow they'd greet ships from England. They would look for someone to hire as a partner. Tomorrow they'd share their gift of freedom.

CHAPTER 9

Women and Work

LIFE IN colonial times wasn't easy for most people. And life for women may have been hardest.

Women had fewer choices. Schools were meant for boys. Rich families sent their sons to college. The finest families sent their sons to England for college.

Girls learned some reading and writing at Dame School. It was like an elementary school. Then girls were finished with schooling. If their parents thought they should learn more, they would teach the girls at home.

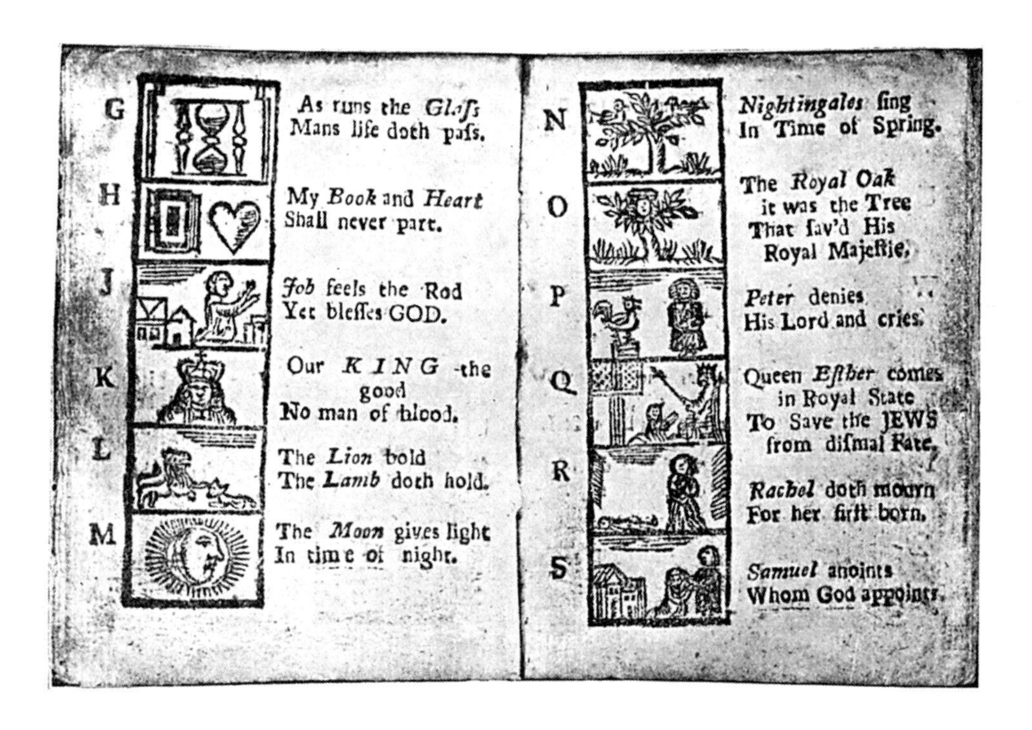
G As runs the *Glaſs*
Mans life doth paſs.

H My *Book* and *Heart*
Shall never part.

J *Job* feels the Rod
Yet bleſſes GOD.

K Our *KING* the good
No man of blood.

L The *Lion* bold
The *Lamb* doth hold.

M The *Moon* gives light
In time of night.

N *Nightingales* ſing
In Time of Spring.

O The *Royal Oak*
it was the Tree
That ſav'd His
Royal Majeſtie.

P *Peter* denies
His Lord and cries.

Q Queen *Eſther* comes
in Royal State
To Save the JEWS
from diſmal Fate.

R *Rachel* doth mourn
For her firſt born.

S *Samuel* anoints
Whom God appoints.

THE FARMER's WIFE

or

THE COMPLETE

COUNTRY HOUSEWIFE.

CONTAINING

Full and ample DIRECTIONS for the Breeding and Management of TURKIES, FOWLS, GEESE, DUCKS, PIGEONS, &c.
INSTRUCTIONS for fattening HOGS, pickling of PORK, and curing of BACON.
How to make SAUSAGES, HOGS-PUDDINGS, &c.
Full INSTRUCTIONS for making WINES from various Kinds of English Fruits, and from Smyrna Raisins.
The METHOD of making CYDER, PERRY, MEAD, MUM, CHERRY-BRANDY, &c.
DIRECTIONS respecting the DAIRY, containing the best Way of making BUTTER, and likewise *Gloucestershire, Cheshire, Stilton, Sage*, and *Cream* CHEESE.
How to pickle common English FRUITS and VEGETABLES, with other useful Receipts for the Country HOUSE-KEEPER.
Full INSTRUCTIONS how to brew BEER and ALE, of all the various Kinds made in this Kingdom.
Ample DIRECTIONS respecting the Management of BEES, with an Account of the Use of HONEY.

To which is added

The Art of Breeding and Managing SONG BIRDS:

Likewise a Variety of RECEIPTS in COOKERY,

And other Particulars, well worthy the Attention of Women of all Ranks residing in the COUNTRY.

Instructions, full and plain, we give,
To teach the Farmer's Wife,
With Satisfaction, how to live
The happy Country Life.

LONDON,

Printed for ALEX. HOGG, in Pater-noster Row.

(Price One Shilling and Six-pence.)

People planned for girls to grow up to be wives and mothers. Their jobs would be at home. They would cook, clean, and watch children.

Fathers with farms or businesses would leave their land or riches to their sons. Fathers hoped their daughters would marry. Then sons-in-law could take over the businesses or farms.

The common choice for a young woman was to marry. But what happened when a husband died? How could the woman earn a living for herself and her children? Were there any choices besides marrying again or living with relatives?

Becoming an indentured servant might have been one of the few choices offered. People from England would agree to work five to seven years if someone would pay for their ship travel to America.

Virginia gave colonists 50 acres of land for each person's passage they paid for. So instead of paying for land, a colonist could pay for more workers.

This was not slavery. An indentured servant signed an agreement to work a limited number of years.

Someone who already lived in America might become an indentured servant if he or she had to repay money owed. Others might be ordered by a judge to work as an indentured servant instead of going to jail.

Indentured servants from England got sick a lot. They were not used to many of the diseases in this country. Many died within two years after arriving in America.

An American like Abigail Alexander would have seemed stronger than an English worker. Also many women died having babies. So a woman who had lived through several childbirths would seem healthier.

However, there were real-life successes for women in the colonial times. Sybilla Masters did invent a corn grinder. A **patent** for her invention was filed in 1715. This gave her the right to make money from the idea.

Sybilla Masters was the first woman in America to gain a patent. Ideas and hope were the best ways to a better life for women back then.

A **patent** is a government document that gives only an inventor the right to make, use, or sell his or her invention.

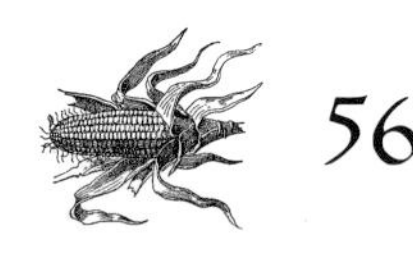

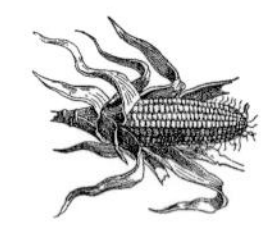